W9-CBY-024

My Robot

My Robot

Eve Bunting
Illustrated by Dagmar Fehlau

Green Light Readers
Harcourt, Inc.
Orlando Austin New York San Diego Toronto London

I got a new robot for my birthday.
I call him Cecil.

Ever since I got him, we have been doing lots of things together.

Cecil plays tag with the children at school. *Whir! Whir!* We hear the sound of his wheels spinning as he races after us. Sometimes he goes a little too fast.

Crash! Smash! Cecil hits the fence. "Not the fence, Cecil!" I call. It's hard not to laugh. Playing tag is not the best thing my robot can do.

All my friends at school like Cecil a lot. He helps our teacher, Mr. Spencer. Helping Mr. Spencer is not the best thing my robot can do.

Cecil leads the school band.
Rum-a-tum-tum. Hear that drum.
"Don't dance, Cecil!" I say. "Don't prance! Just march!" Leading the band is not the best thing my robot can do.

Cecil picks me up after school.
He gives me a ride home.
"How's the weather up there?"my little brother
Dennis asks. He gets a ride home, too.

Once in a while, Cecil does tricks with our dog, Prince. They can roll over. *Whirl! Whirl!* They can beg. *Creak! Fizz! Whiz!* "Shake, Prince," says Dennis. "Shake, Cecil!" Doing tricks is not the best thing my robot can do.

Cecil plays hide-and-seek, too. He is always IT. He gives everyone a chance to find a good place to hide.

Clank! Clunk! Here comes Cecil!
We don't say we heard him coming. He whistles when he finds us. *Whir! Spark! Pop!* Playing hide-and-seek is not the best thing my robot can do.

Everyone has heard about Cecil's cakes.
He makes circus animals with the frosting.
His cakes are almost too pretty to eat.
"This is your best cake yet!" says Dennis.

“Cecil’s cakes are pretty good,” I say, “but that is still not the best thing my robot can do.”
“My tummy tells me it is,” Dennis says.

Cecil can mow the grass. *Whir! Wheeze! Whish!* Cecil goes very fast. It's a hot day, but Dad is not hot.

"This MUST be the best thing Cecil can do," says Dad.
"Almost," I tell Dad. "You and Dennis come with me. I'll show you something else Cecil can do."

“Look in here. Even cleaning my room is not the best thing my robot can do.” I give Cecil a hug.

"Thanks, Cecil," I whisper. "The very best thing you can do is be my friend!"
Flash! Spark! Whirl! Pop!
Cecil knows.

ACTIVITY

Ready Robot Puppets

If you had a robot, how would your robot help you? Make a robot puppet and act out all the ways it could help.

WHAT YOU'LL NEED

a cardboard tube or rolled-up paper

tape

glue

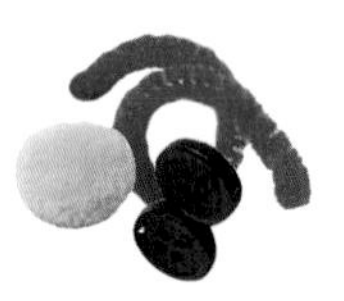
collage materials

construction paper

markers or crayons

1. Use the tube for the robot's body. Draw a face on the tube.

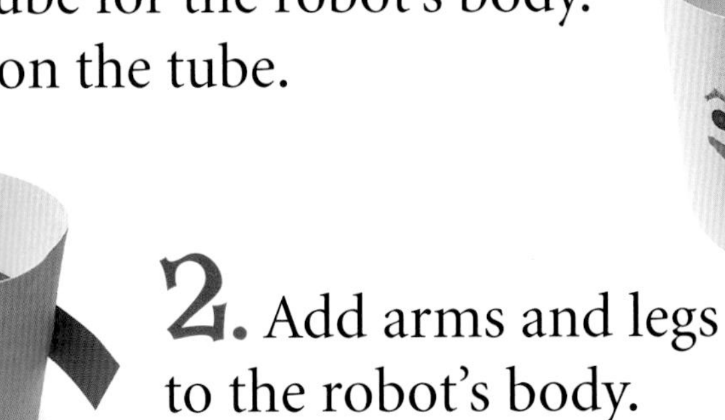

2. Add arms and legs to the robot's body.

3. Decorate your robot. Think of things you would like your robot to do for you.

Use your creation to show how a robot could help you.

Meet the Author and Illustrator

Eve Bunting once met a robot. Students had made him out of cardboard. He was a great robot! She thought about how grand it would be to have her very own robot. Then she decided to write this story about it! She is very happy to share *My Robot* with you.

Eve Bunting

Dagmar Fehlau was born in Germany, and then came to the United States to study art. She always loved drawing and painting, so she knew she would be an artist when she grew up. She hopes you like the pictures in *My Robot*.

Dagmar Fehlau

www.HarcourtBooks.com

First Green Light Readers edition 2006

Library of Congress Cataloging-in-Publication Data
Bunting, Eve, 1928–
My robot/by Eve Bunting; illustrated by Dagmar Fehlau.
p. cm.
"Green Light Readers."
Summary: Cecil the robot is good at playing tag, leading the school band, and performing tricks with the dog, but there is one important thing he does best of all.
[1. Automata—Fiction. 2. Friendship—Fiction.]
I. Fehlau, Dagmar, ill. II. Title. III. Series.
PZ7.B91527Myr 2006
[E]—dc22 2005006936
ISBN-13: 978-0152-05593-6 ISBN-10: 0-15-205593-2
ISBN-13: 978-0152-05617-9 (pb) ISBN-10: 0-15-205617-3 (pb)

A C E G H F D B
A C E G H F D B (pb)

Ages 5–7
Grades: 1
Guided Reading Level: G–H
Reading Recovery Level: 12–13

"A must-have for any family with a beginning reader."—*Boston Sunday Herald*

"You can't go wrong with adding several copies of these terrific books to your beginning-to-read collection."—*School Library Journal*

"A winner for the beginner."—*Booklist*

Five Tips to Help Your Child Become a Great Reader

1. Get involved. Reading aloud to and with your child is just as important as encouraging your child to read independently.

2. Be curious. Ask questions about what your child is reading.

3. Make reading fun. Allow your child to pick books on subjects that interest her or him.

4. Words are everywhere—not just in books. Practice reading signs, packages, and cereal boxes with your child.

5. Set a good example. Make sure your child sees YOU reading.

Why Green Light Readers Is the Best Series for Your New Reader

- Created exclusively for beginning readers by some of the biggest and brightest names in children's books
- Reinforces the reading skills your child is learning in school
- Encourages children to read—and finish—books by themselves
- Offers extra enrichment through fun, age-appropriate activities unique to each story
- Incorporates characteristics of the Reading Recovery program used by educators
- Developed with Harcourt School Publishers and credentialed educational consultants

LEVEL

2 Start the Engine! Reading with Help

Daniel's Mystery Egg
Alma Flor Ada/G. Brian Karas

Moving Day
Anthony G. Brandon/Wong Herbert Yee

My Robot
Eve Bunting/Dagmar Fehlau

Animals on the Go
Jessica Brett/Richard Cowdrey

Marco's Run
Wesley Cartier/Reynold Ruffins

Digger Pig and the Turnip
Caron Lee Cohen/Christopher Denise

Tumbleweed Stew
Susan Stevens Crummel/Janet Stevens

The Chick That Wouldn't Hatch
Claire Daniel/Lisa Campbell Ernst

Splash!
Ariane Dewey/Jose Aruego

Get That Pest!
Erin Douglas/Wong Herbert Yee

My Wild Woolly
Deborah J. Eaton/G. Brian Karas

A Place for Nicholas
Lucy Floyd/David McPhail

Why the Frog Has Big Eyes
Betsy Franco/Joung Un Kim

I Wonder
Tana Hoban

A Bed Full of Cats
Holly Keller

The Fox and the Stork
Gerald McDermott

Try Your Best
Robert McKissack/Joe Cepeda

Lucy's Quiet Book
Angela Shelf Medearis/Lisa Campbell Ernst

On the Way to the Pond
Angela Shelf Medearis/Lorinda Bryan Cauley

Tomás Rivera
Jane Medina/Edward Martinez

Boots for Beth
Alex Moran/Lisa Campbell Ernst

Catch Me If You Can!
Bernard Most

The Very Boastful Kangaroo
Bernard Most

Skimper-Scamper
Jeff Newell/Barbara Hranilovich

Farmers Market
Carmen Parks/Edward Martinez

Shoe Town
Janet Stevens/Susan Stevens Crummel

The Enormous Turnip
Alexei Tolstoy/Scott Goto

Where Do Frogs Come From?
Alex Vern

The Purple Snerd
Rozanne Lanczak Williams/Mary GrandPré

Did You See Chip?
Wong Herbert Yee/Laura Ovresat

Look for more Green Light Readers wherever books are sold!